Greenwillow
Read-alone

BUFFY and

ALBERT

by Charlotte Pomerantz
pictures by Yossi Abolafia

Greenwillow Books, New York

Library of Congress Cataloging in Publication Data
Pomerantz, Charlotte.   Buffy and Albert.
(Greenwillow read-alone books)
Summary: While recovering from a twisted ankle, Grandpa's
feelings about his two elderly cats change.
[1. Old age–Fiction.   2. Cats–Fiction.   3. Grandfathers–Fiction]
I. Abolafia, Yossi, ill.   II. Title.   III. Series.
PZ7.P77Bu   [E]   81-20144
ISBN 0-688-00920-4   AACR2
ISBN 0-688-00921-2 (lib. bdg.)

FOR MY BROTHER DANIEL
—C.P.

My grandfather is old.

He lives with two very old cats.

Their names are Buffy and Albert.

Buffy is light brown,

except for her nose and paws.

They are white.

Albert is black,

except for his whiskers.

They are gray.

Grandpa has three children.

They are all grown up,

like my father.

They live in their own homes.

He also has two grandchildren–
my brother and me.
So my grandfather is a father
to my father
and a grandfather to me.

Grandpa says he can remember
when he was younger
than my father is now.
And my father
was even younger
than I am!

Then, Grandpa says,

the house was full of noise

and stuffed animals and kittens.

It was full of sneakers

and schoolbooks

and giggly sounds.

Now the house is quiet.

Grandpa likes it that way.

He has time to read

lots of books

and carve things out of wood.

Sometimes he visits us.

Sometimes we visit him.

He says he likes to live alone.

He says he would even like to live

without Buffy and Albert.

But they are so used to him,

they wouldn't be happy

anywhere else.

One day, after school,

my brother and I came over.

Grandpa made us cocoa.

He put two marshmallows

in each cup.

We sat next to the cats

and patted their fur

and listened to them purr.

"Nice old Buffy,

big and fluffy," I said.

"Nice old Albert,"

said my brother.

He couldn't think of a rhyme.

15

I asked Grandpa,

"How old would Buffy and Albert be

if they were people?"

"Let's see," said Grandpa.

"One year in the life of a cat

is about seven in the life

of a human being.

So Buffy is 91.

And Albert

is 112 years old."

"Wow!" said

my brother.

"They *are* old!"

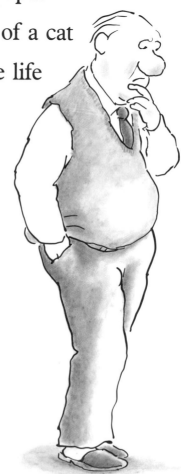

"Old and a bother,"
said Grandpa.
"Albert's legs are so weak
that he can hardly jump up
on the sofa.
He also drools."
"What about Buffy?" I asked.
"Buffy snores," said Grandpa.
"And sometimes she pees
on the floor."

"I wish we could take them home,"
said my brother.

Grandpa's face lit up.

"Why don't you?"

"We can't," I said.

"Our dog doesn't like cats."

"Neither do I," said Grandpa.

My brother asked,

"Did you like Buffy and Albert

when they were kittens?"

"Of course," said Grandpa.

"But as a poet said,

'The trouble with a kitten is

THAT

Eventually it becomes a

CAT.' "

Next time I visited Grandpa,

Albert drooled on a library book.

Buffy peed on a wood carving.

"Thunderation!" exclaimed Grandpa.

He put the cats in their basket.

He put the basket
on the back of his bicycle
and rode to town.
I followed.

Dr. Koshka was glad to see us.

"Well, if it isn't Buffy and Albert,"
he said.

"They must be 100 years old."

"More like 200," said Grandpa.

"Aw, Grandpa," I said,

"Buffy is only 91."

"What's the matter with them?"
said Dr. Koshka.
"Everything," said Grandpa.
"They are old and a bother."
Dr. Koshka examined them.

"It's nothing serious," he said.
"Just put these vitamins
   in their cat food.
   With a little care,
   they may live for years."
"Years!" exclaimed Grandpa.

When we got back,

Buffy and Albert fell asleep.

Grandpa sat down to read a book.

I went to get some cookies.

Suddenly there was a noise.

An arm of Grandpa's chair

had come loose.

He had fallen to the floor

and he was in pain.

He was yelling at Buffy and Albert,

"Good-for-nothing-old cats!

You can't even call for help."

I ran to him.

"Don't worry, Grandpa," I said.

"I'm here."

I put a blanket over him
and called our doctor.

The doctor told Grandpa,
"You have twisted your ankle.
You must stay off your leg
for a week."

The whole family took turns
taking care of Grandpa.
My brother and I
came every day after school.

My mother shopped and cooked.
My father did the laundry
and folded it.

We all took turns
washing the dishes
and emptying the garbage.
My brother and I
fed the cats.
We didn't forget the vitamins.

We also made our own cocoa

and put three marshmallows

in each cup.

We sat next to Buffy and Albert.

We patted their fur

and listened to them purr.

"Nice old Buffy,

big and fluffy," I said.

"Nice old Albert,"

said my brother.

He could never think of a rhyme.

Grandpa lay in bed
and smiled at us.
Sometimes he had
a funny faraway look.
Maybe he was thinking about
what he was going to carve
when he felt better.

I brought him his dinner.

"I'm sorry to be such a bother,"
he said.

"You're not a bother," I said.

"I like taking care of you."

We heard my brother
in the next room.
"Uh-oh. Buffy peed
on the rug."
Grandpa put down his fork.
"Stupid old cat!" he said.

My brother stood at the door.

He was crying.

"Don't talk to Buffy that way,"
he said.

"She can't help it if she's old."

Grandpa sighed.

"You're right," he said.

"Everybody gets old."

My brother and I

looked at each other.

"You're not old, Grandpa,"
  I said.
"Yes, I am," said Grandpa.
"No, you're not,"
  said my brother.
"Buffy and Albert are lots older."
  Grandpa chuckled.
"That's true," he said.

After a week, Grandpa was all right.

He could take care of himself.

He thanked us

for taking such good care of him.

The next day I came to see him.

Grandpa was fixing

the arm of his chair.

"I'll hold the arm in place,"

he said.

"You hammer in the nails."

When the chair was fixed,

he tested it.

Then he went to his table
and began to carve.
I wondered if he was glad
that the house was quiet again.
He must have read my thoughts.

"Last night," he said,
"I just lay in bed
and listened to the quiet.
Buffy jumped up.
Her warm body felt good
against my ankle.
Albert tried to jump up too.
He couldn't jump high enough.
His old legs were too weak.
But on the third try,
he made it."

I put my arms around Grandpa
and hugged him.
Then I tried to figure out
what he was carving.
I wasn't sure–
"Grandpa, it almost looks like..."

"You're right," said Grandpa.

"It's a cat."

CHARLOTTE POMERANTZ was born in New York City, where she lives with her husband, Carl Marzani, and their two children. Among the many well-loved books she has written are *If I Had a Paka: Poems in Eleven Languages*, *The Tamarindo Puppy*, an A.L.A. Notable Book, and *The Mango Tooth*.

YOSSI ABOLAFIA was born in Tiberia, Israel. He has worked as a film animator and is the illustrator of four children's books published in Israel. He is presently director of animation for The National Film Board of Canada.